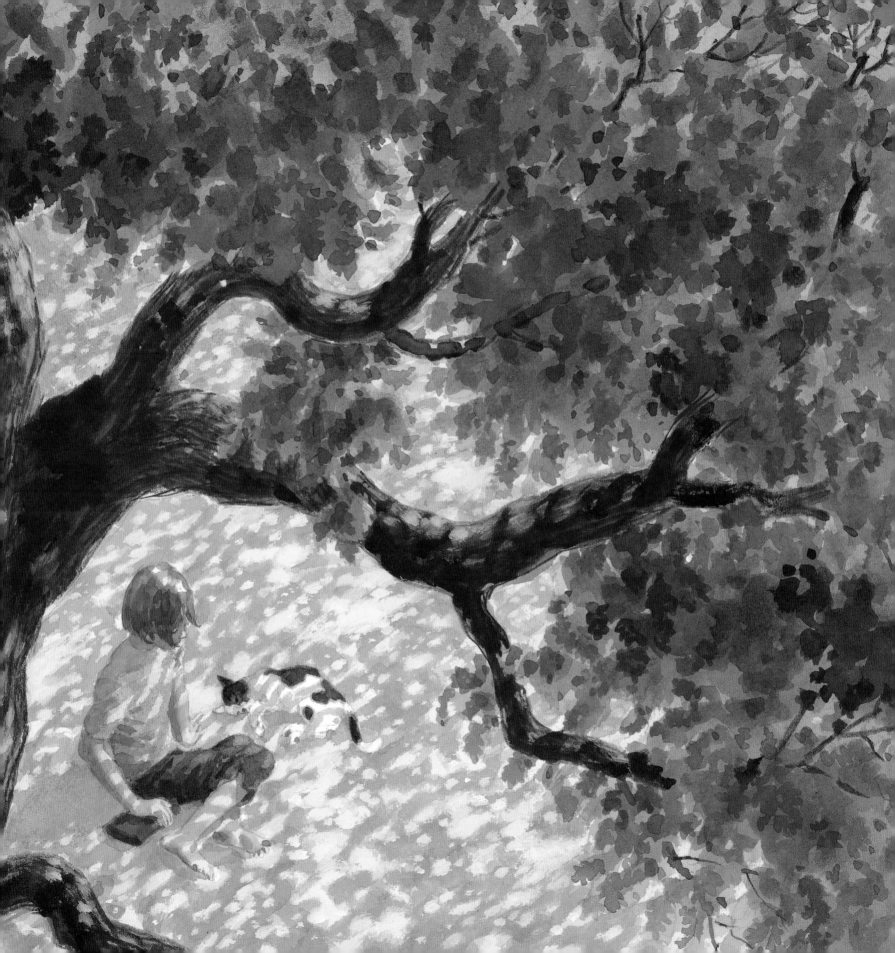

The
Memory String

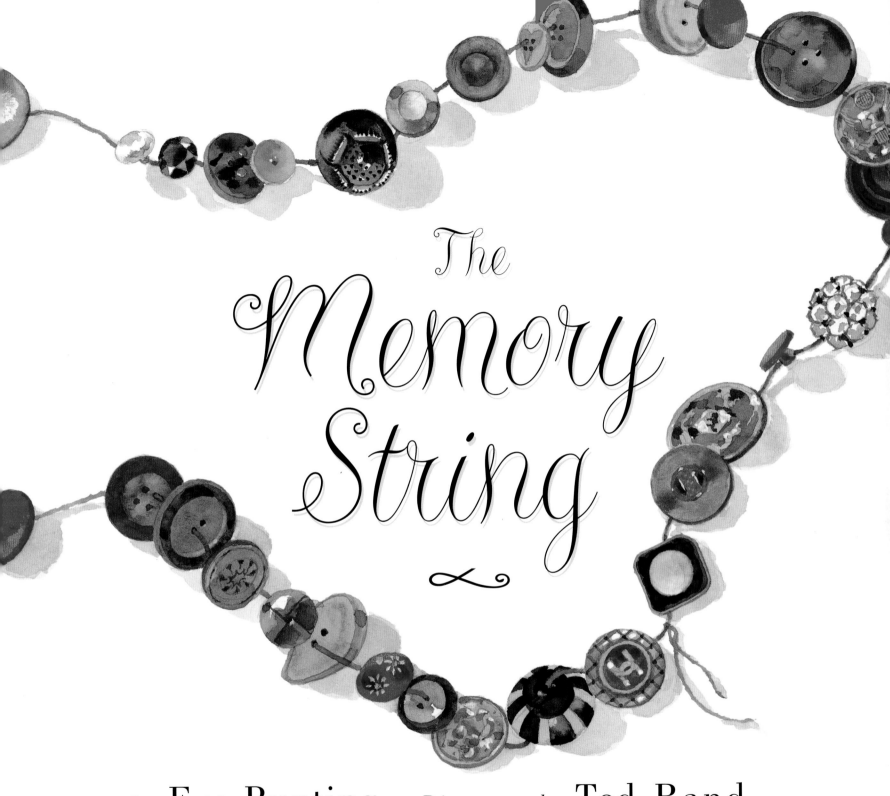

The Memory String

by Eve Bunting ○ Pictures by Ted Rand

Houghton Mifflin Harcourt
Boston New York

All rights reserved. Originally published in hardcover in the United States by Clarion Books, an imprint of Houghton Mifflin Harcourt
Publishing Company, 2000.

For information about permission to reproduce selections from this book, write to Permissions, Houghton Mifflin Harcourt
Publishing Company, 215 Park Avenue South, New York, New York 10003.

www.hmhco.com

The text for this book was set in Bodoni.
The illustrations were executed in watercolor.

The Library of Congress has cataloged the hardcover edition as follows:
Bunting, Eve, 1928–
The memory string / Eve Bunting ; illustrated by Ted Rand.
p.   cm.
Summary: While still grieving for her mother and unable to accept her stepmother,
a girl clings to the memories represented by forty-three buttons on a string.
[1. Memory—Fiction. 2. Stepmothers—Fiction. 3. Grief—Fiction.]
I. Rand, Ted, ill. II. Title.
PZ7.B91527Me 2000
[E]—dc21   99-42771

ISBN: 978-0-395-86146-2 hardcover
ISBN: 978-0-544-55547-1 paperback

Manufactured in China
SCP 10 9 8 7 6 5 4 3 2 1

4500531820

To Ernie,
who will always be on my memory string
—E.B.

To Merideth and her children,
Della, Alia, Ramsey, Zane and Jenna
—T.R.

Laura sat under the oak tree in their small back yard. Whiskers, her black-and-white cat, lay beside her, twitching his tail. On the porch her dad and her new stepmother, Jane, were painting the railings.

Jane stopped and pushed her hair away from her face. She wore an old paint-stained shirt and skinny-leg jeans.

"Want some lemonade?" she called.

Laura shook her head. While Jane was still looking in her direction, she took the memory string from the red velvet box on her lap. The buttons strung on the string shone and silvered, patterned with oak-leaf shadows.

Jane dipped her brush in the paint and went back to work. Her shoulders were stiff. Laura had pulled out this string a lot in front of her stepmother.

"This was my great-grandmother's memory string," Laura told Whiskers in a loud voice. "Then it was my grandmother's, then my mother's, and now it's mine."

"Are you sure you don't want some lemonade?" her dad called.

"No thanks," Laura said.

"If you're not doing anything important, you might come and help us." Jane's voice was sharp.

"I *am* doing something important," Laura said.

"This button came off my great-grandmother's first grown-up dress," she told Whiskers. "Back then some people couldn't read, or keep diaries, so a string like this was their way to remember. Mom told me."

Whiskers yawned.

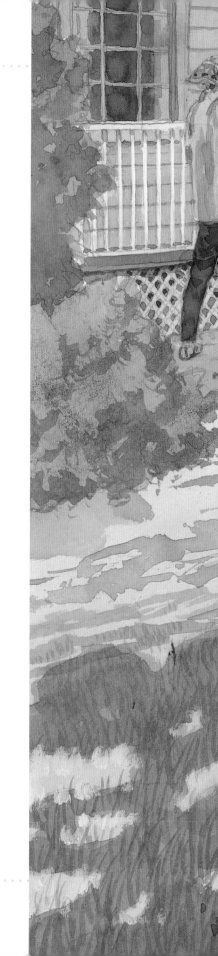

"This button was my great-aunt's. She wore the dress to a quilting party. It's all part of our family's history."

Whiskers got up to leave, but Laura took a firm grip under his stomach and crushed him against her, leaving her arms free.

"Yowww!" Whiskers warned.

"Be quiet," Laura whispered. "I can't talk about my memory string to myself, can I? You have to stay here."

"These three buttons were from second cousins of my grandma's. The cousins were at a spelling bee." She peered up under her bangs. Dad was pouring lemonade. He took a frosted glass to Jane, and she sat back on her heels and smiled at him.

Laura saw him touch Jane's neck, under her hair. He did that often. Sometimes Dad and Jane sat on the porch at night after Laura had gone to bed. Her room was above, and she'd hear them whispering and laughing softly. They seemed so happy. It hurt to hear them happy like that.

She rubbed the buttons between her fingers. Get to the good parts, she thought. Forget the cousins. Get to Mom.

"This button came from Mom's prom dress," she told Whiskers. "Stop squirming," she added. "And this is from her wedding dress. It was white, of course.

"And see this little teeny tiny one? This is off my christening dress, and this one is off the dress I wore to my fifth birthday party. I remember."

She stopped for breath and glanced up again at Jane. All this must hurt her a lot. For an instant Laura felt mean and horrible. But only for an instant. She didn't *hate* Jane. Not really. It was just that Jane had gone and married Dad.

She had to rush now, because Dad was coming down the front steps. "This khaki one was off Dad's uniform when he went to war in a place called the Gulf. Mom cut it off his jacket when he came home, and she cried and cried because she was so happy he was safe."

Dad stood in front of her, bare ankles, old torn tennies. "Laura . . . ?"

Quickly, before he could stop her, Laura said, "This last one fastened the neck of Mom's nightgown, the one she was wearing when she died. Dad saved it for me." She held up the memory string. It turned, the colors blurring through the blur in her eyes.

Whiskers leapt.

"Watch it!" Dad said anxiously. But he was too late.

Whiskers's claws caught on the string, scattering buttons like sunflower seeds.

Laura covered her eyes with her hands. "Oh, no!"

Up on the porch, Jane dropped the paintbrush and rushed down the steps. "It's okay, sweetie," she said. "We'll find them."

The three of them searched the grass.

"I've found one," Dad said.

"Here's another," Jane called.

Whiskers watched from the top of the sagging fence.

"Bad Whiskers!" One by one Laura put the buttons carefully back in the box. "There were forty-three," she said. "I'm still missing seven."

They found six more. Their knees were covered with dirt. Ants crawled over their hands and arms.

They sifted through leaves and dead blossoms that had blown off the camellia bushes by the porch. "Do you know which one is still missing?" Jane asked.

"The one from Dad's uniform. It was Mom's favorite, because . . . because . . ."

Tears streamed down Laura's face, and Jane took a step toward her. "Oh, Laura, my dear."

It was what Mom would have said. What Mom would have done. Jane's voice was soft, as Mom's would have been. But this wasn't Mom. Mom had died three years ago. This was Jane.

"Dad?" Laura whispered, and her dad folded her against him.

They searched again after supper until the light faded while Whiskers lay on the porch, lazily swatting bugs.

25

When she finally went to bed, Laura couldn't sleep.

"We'll find the button in the morning," Dad had promised.

"And I'll help you restring them," Jane said.

"Thanks. But I know how to do it," Laura told her.

She lay, listening to the crickets, listening to Whiskers purring beside her.

A little later she heard the murmur of porch voices, and she got out of bed and knelt by the window.

Jane and Dad sat in the swing. She could hear its soft creak. Bugs batted against the yellow light bulb.

"But there won't be any difference," Dad was saying. "My old uniform is in one of those boxes we stored in the attic. I can cut a button off and drop it in the grass. She'll never know."

"How can you think of such a thing?" Jane asked. "Those are true moments on that string. You can't cheat Laura like that."

"But, sweetheart." Laura imagined Dad taking off his baseball cap, rubbing his head the way he did when he was worried. "My little girl's heart is breaking. I only want to make her feel better."

"Laura would rather have that button missing than have a replacement," Jane said. And then she added, "It's like a mother. No substitute allowed."

Laura heard the chokiness in Jane's voice. She felt choked up herself.

The swing squeaked as one of them stood up. "Let's look some more. Right now," Jane said.

"Now? You can't see a thing."

"Flashlights," Jane said.

Laura bit her lip. Should she go, too? But then they'd know she'd heard.

She watched the white circles of the flashlights, the dark figures of Jane and Dad crawling through the grass. She could smell the fresh paint. The crickets had stopped singing to listen.

And then she heard Jane's excited voice. "I found it. Over here! It must have rolled." She held something up between her finger and thumb.

"Whoopee!" Dad swung Jane round and round and Jane laughed. "Careful! We don't want to lose it again!"

"She'll be so happy! You can give it to her at breakfast, Janie."

"I don't think so," Jane said, "She won't like it that I'm the one who found it. Let's just leave it on the porch. Like a gift from a good fairy."

Laura got slowly back into bed. Whiskers had moved into her warm place, and she slid him over.

"Grr!" he warned.

She lay, thinking. Jane's sad voice saying: "It's like a mother. No substitute allowed." She remembered the soft look on Jane's face today. The way she had understood about the true moments on the string.

So much to think about. So much.

As soon as she wakened the next morning, Laura went downstairs. Jane was painting the back door robin's-egg blue. "Like it?" she asked.

Laura nodded. Already she could see the button on the porch. She picked it up and held it tight in her hand. "A good fairy must have brought it," she said.

She noticed that the buttons on Jane's painting shirt were a deep, dark green. Pretty! Maybe one day she'd ask Jane for one to put on the memory string.

She swallowed. "Will you really help me restring them, Jane?"

Jane wiped her hands on a rag and stood up. "Anytime you want," she said. "I'm here."

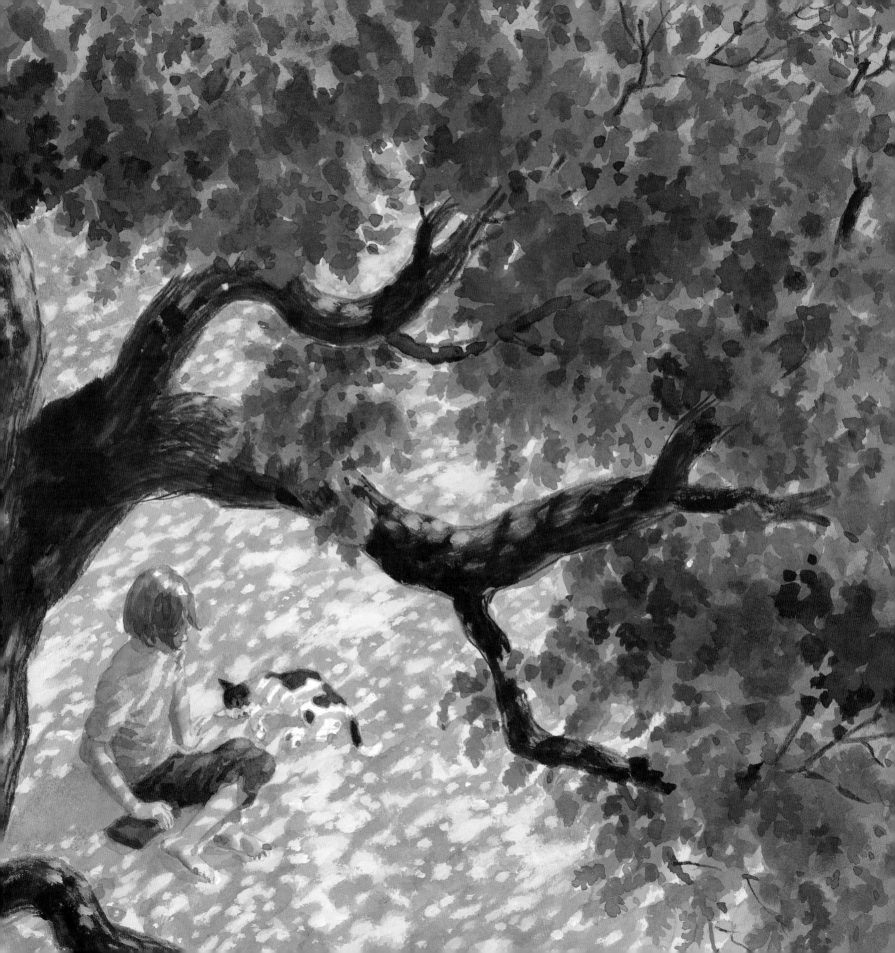

Eve Bunting is the beloved author of more than two hundred books for young children and middle grade readers. Among her many popular picture books are *The Wall*, *Fly Away Home*, and *Train to Somewhere*. Ms. Bunting lives in Pasadena, California.

Ted Rand is the esteemed illustrator of many picture books, including Eve Bunting's *Secret Place*. He lives on Mercer Island, Washington.

Other Picture Books by Eve Bunting